ASPIRIN

Alan Trussell-Cullen

Australia • Brazil • Japan • Korea • Mexico • Singapore • Spain • United Kingdom • United States

Aspirin

Fast Forward
Level 13

Text: Alan Trussell-Cullen
Editor: Cameron Macintosh
Designer: Stella Vassiliou
Illustrations : Boris Silvestri
Series Designer: James Lowe
Production Controller: Emma Hayes
Photo Research: Gillian Cardinal
Audio recordings: Juliet Hill, Picture Start

Speakers: Matthew King and Abbe Holmes
Reprint: Jennifer Foo

Acknowledgements
The author and publisher would like to acknowledge permission to reproduce material from the following sources: Photographs by Australian Picture Library/Corbis/Bettmann, p. 20; Bayer, p. 16; Masterfile/Steve Craft, p. 5; PhotoEdit/Rachel Espstein, cover bottom, pp. 1 bottom, 22/ Tom McCarthy, p. 4; Photolibrary.com/Botanica, p. 6 right/ SPL, p. 12/ Imagestate Ltd, backcover; Science & Society Picture Library/Science Museum, cover centre, pp. 1 centre, 18; The Advertising Archives, pp. 21, 23 bottom.

Originally published in Australia in 2007

ISBN 978 0 17 012578 9
ISBN 978 0 17 012573 4 (set)

Cengage Learning Australia
Level 7, 80 Dorcas Street
South Melbourne, Victoria Australia 3205
Phone: 1300 790 853

Cengage Learning New Zealand
Unit 4B Rosedale Office Park
331 Rosedale Road, Albany, North Shore NZ 0632
Phone: 0800 449 725

For learning solutions, visit **cengage.com.au**

Printed in Australia by Ligare Pty Limited
10 11 12 13 14 15 16 23 22 21 20 19

THE UNIVERSITY OF MELBOURNE

Evaluated in independent research by staff from the Department of Language, Literacy and Arts Education at the University of Melbourne.

Alan Trussell-Cullen

Contents

Chapter 1

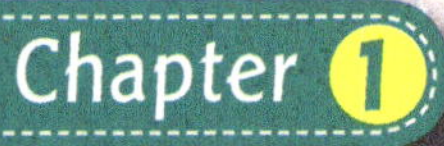

ASPIRIN

Aspirin is the most widely used **medicine** in the world. For over 100 years, people have been taking aspirin:

- when they have a fever
- to help stop headaches
- for other aches and pains.

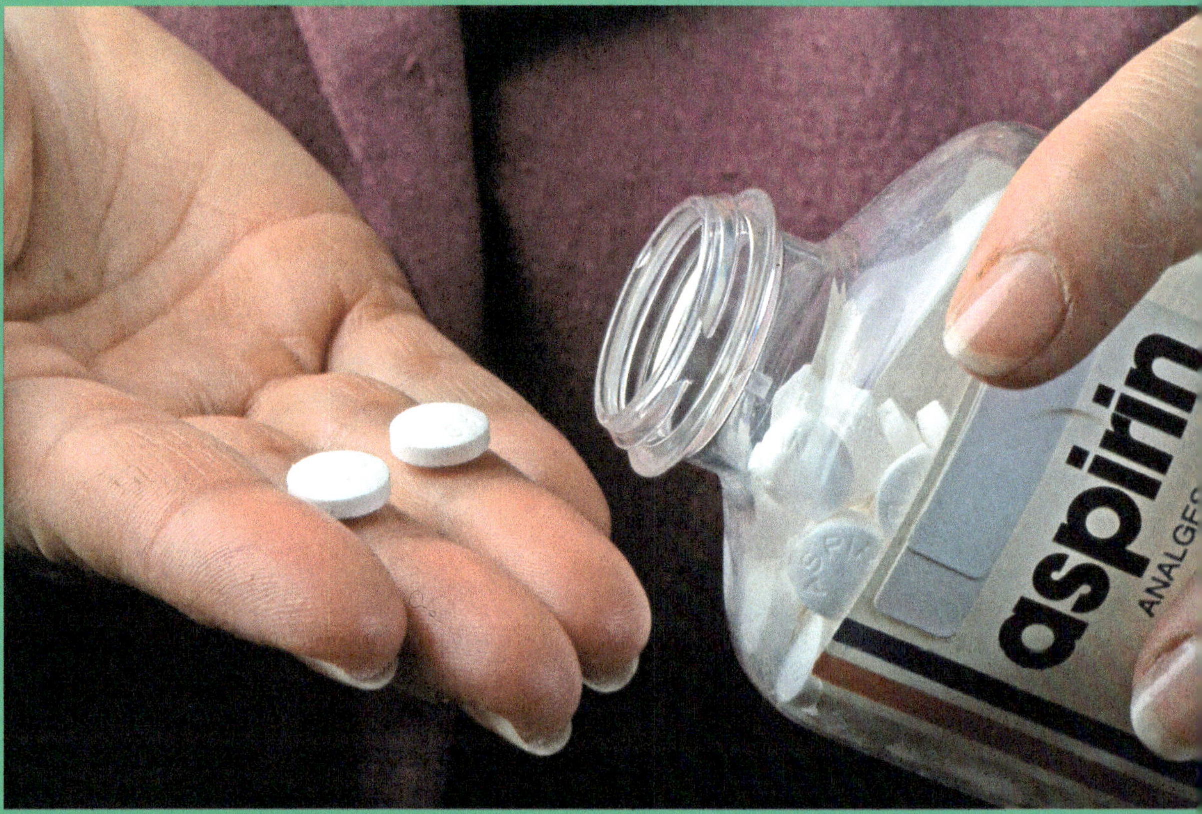

RITE AID
Aspirin
ANALGESIC
NO CAFFEINE
EASY TO SWALLOW
RELIEVES PAIN
100 TABLETS

Chapter 2

WILLOW BARK MEDICINE

Many people have played a part in how aspirin was invented.

For thousands of years, people have been using plants as medicines.
People used to make a medicine from the bark of the willow tree to help with their aches and pains.

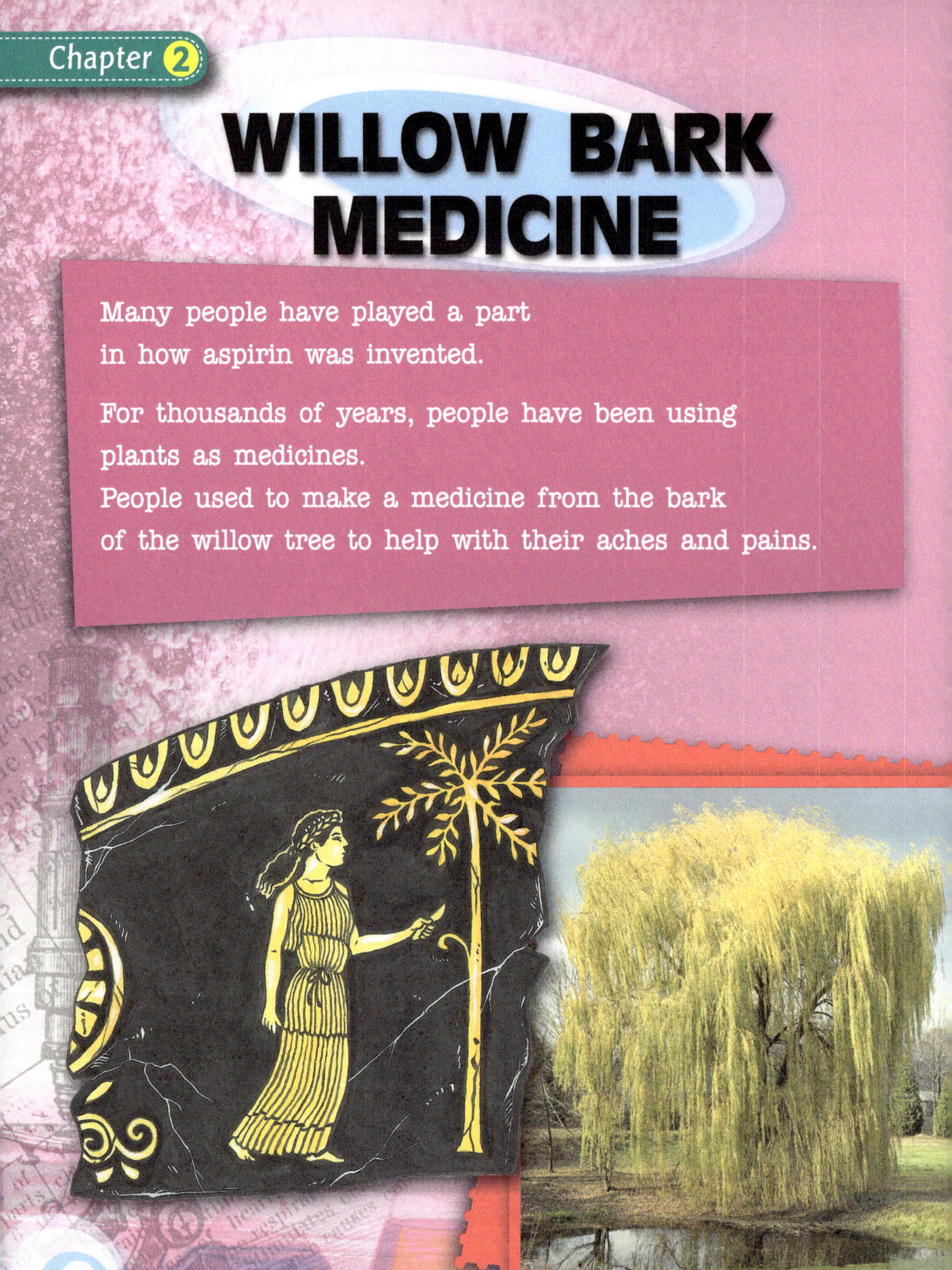

People made a tea with the willow bark. They didn't know how it worked, but they found that it helped pain to go away.

Chapter 3

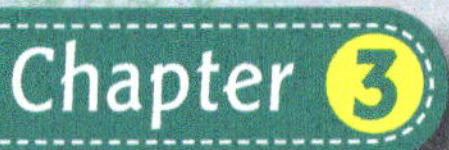

THE YELLOW CHEMICAL

In the 1800s, many **scientists** tried to find out what was in the willow bark that helped stop pain.

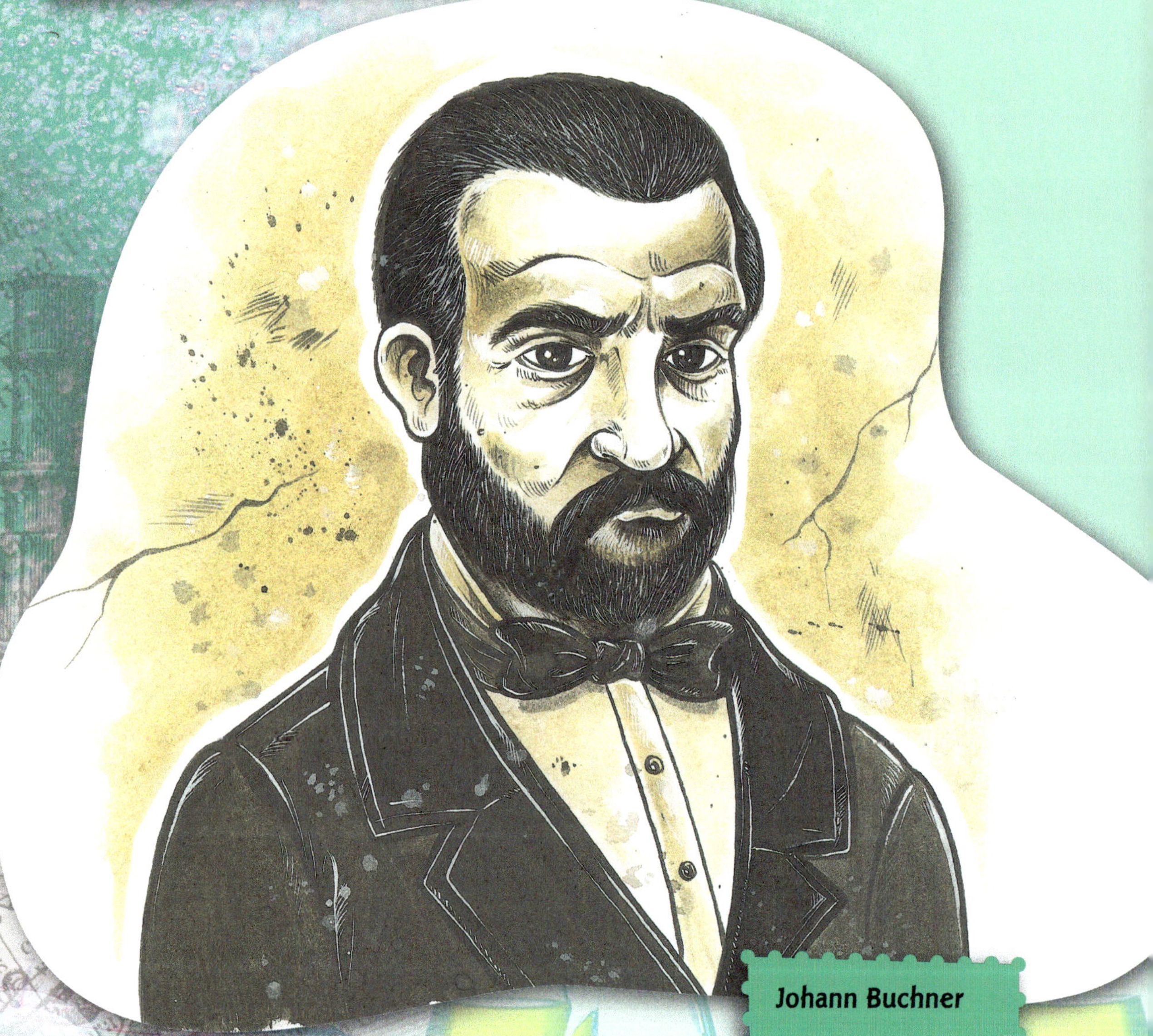

Johann Buchner

willow bark

In 1828, Johann Buchner found that it had a yellow **chemical** in it.
He called this yellow chemical salicin (*say: sal-i-cin*).

Buchner got some people to try his salicin for their headaches.
It worked!
The pain went away.

Running Words 154

The only problem was that the salicin tasted awful, and gave people bad stomach pains.

MAKING IT BETTER

In 1853, Charles Gerhardt added some other chemicals to the salicin.
These chemicals helped to stop the stomach pains.

Charles Gerhardt

Gerhardt believed that his medicine
was too hard to make.
He made lots of notes,
but he didn't do anything with them.

So people kept taking the old salicin mix, and kept having bad stomach pains.

Chapter 5

GERHARDT'S NOTES

In 1883, Felix Hoffman's father was in a lot of pain. Hoffman gave his father a lot of medicines, but nothing helped.

Felix Hoffman

One day, Hoffman found Gerhardt's notes.
He made some of Gerhardt's medicine
for his father.
Hoffman's father took the medicine,
and the pain went away.
The medicine worked!

Chapter 6

FACTORY ASPIRIN

Hoffman worked for a company that made medicines. He told them about Gerhardt's medicine, and in 1898, the factory began to make it. They called the medicine 'aspirin', and they sold it as a powder.

In 1915, aspirin powder was made into a tablet.
This was another great idea!
It was the first medicine to be sold to people as a tablet.
Aspirin was also the first medicine to be advertised.

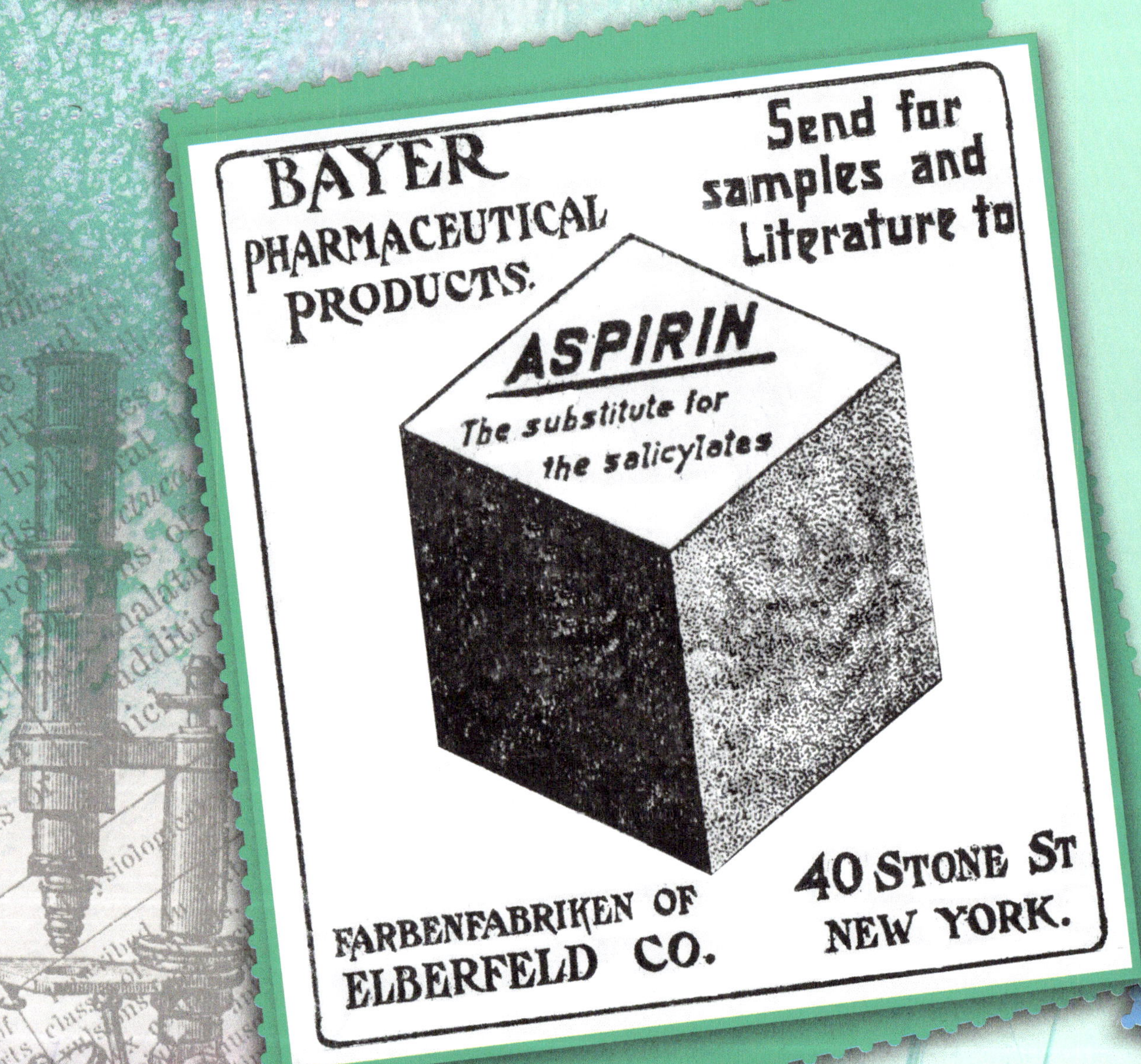

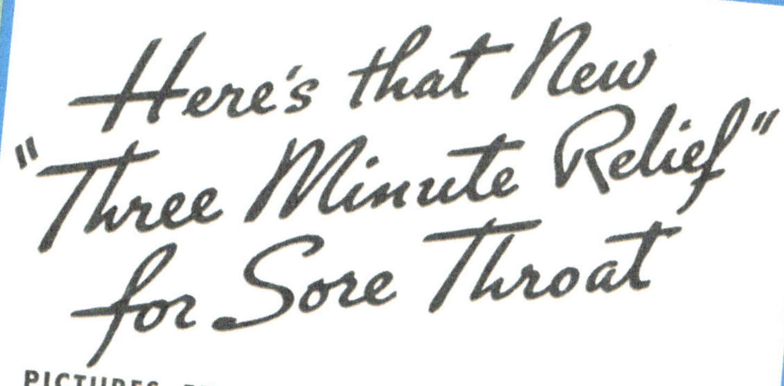

PICTURES EXPLAIN SIMPLE NEW TREATMENT DOCTORS NOW PRESCRIBE

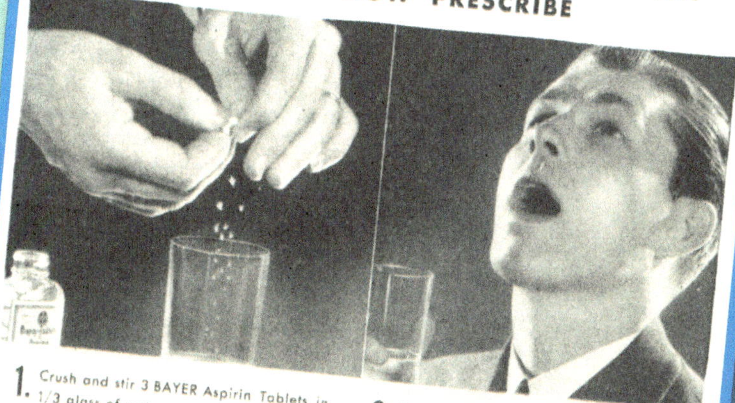

1. Crush and stir 3 BAYER Aspirin Tablets in 1/3 glass of water.

2. Gargle Thoroughly—throw your head way back, allowing a little to trickle down your throat. Do this twice. Do not rinse mouth.

3. If you have a cold, take 2 BAYER Aspirin Tablets. Drink full glass of water. Repeat if necessary according to directions in package.

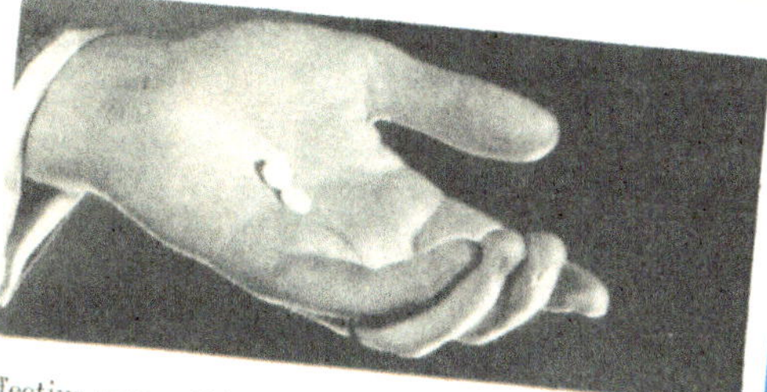

Here's a safe, modern and effective way to relieve sore throat. A way that eases the pain, rawness and irritation in as little as two or three minutes!

Millions are now following this way. Doctors are advising it. Try it. Results are quick and amazing.

Simple To Do

All you do is crush and stir 3 BAYER Aspirin Tablets in a third of a glass of water. Gargle with it twice — as pictured above. (If you have signs of a cold, take BAYER Aspirin Tablets and drink lenty of water.)

Get *real* BAYER Aspirin Tablets for this purpose. They disintegrate completely enough to gargle without leaving irritating particles.

BAYER Aspirin prices have been decisively reduced, so there's no point now in accepting other than the real Bayer article you want.

NOW REDUCED TO

15¢

RICES ON GENUINE BAYER ASPIRIN RADICALLY REDUCED ON ALL SIZES. OTTLE OF 24 TABLETS NOW 25c. BOTTLE OF 100 TABLETS NOW 75c.

Chapter 7

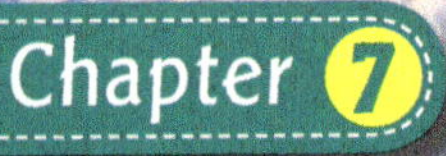

ASPIRIN TODAY

Today, all over the world, one billion aspirin tablets are taken each week!

As well as for pain and fevers,
aspirin is now used for other things,
such as heart problems and some cancers.
It is no wonder aspirin has been called a wonder drug!

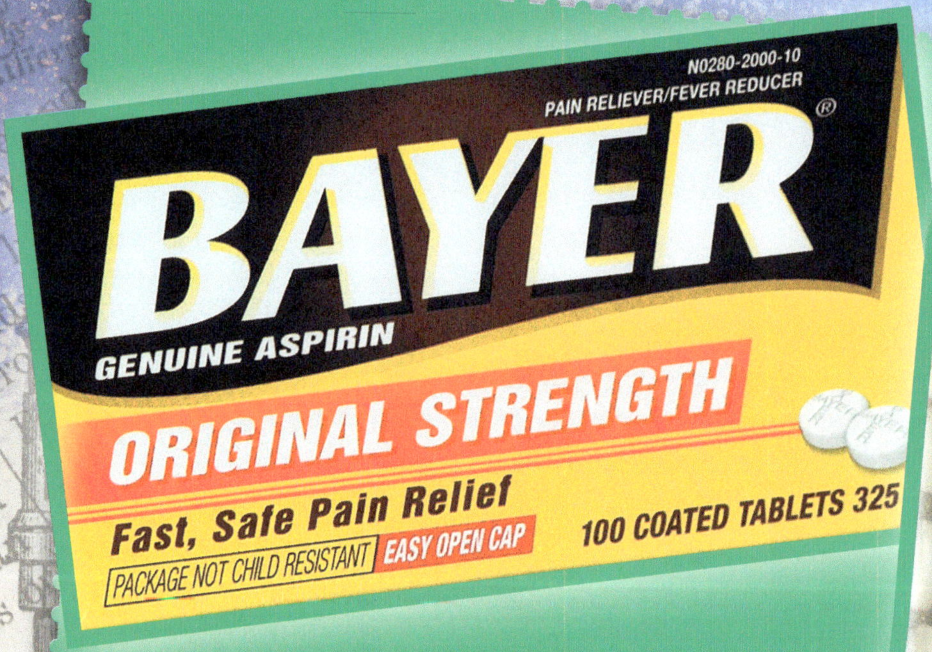

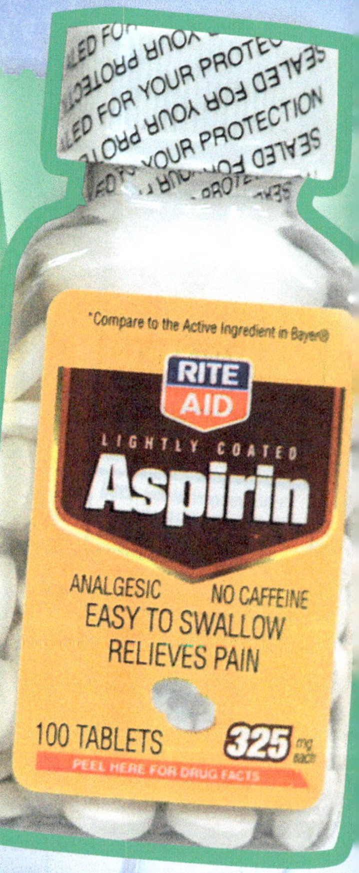

Aspirin Timeline

500 BC

tea made from willow bark

1828

Buchner uses salicin as a medicine

1853

Gerhardt adds chemicals to salicin, to stop people getting stomach pains

1883

Hoffman uses Gerhardt's notes to make medicine

1898

aspirin first used as a powder

1915

aspirin made into a tablet

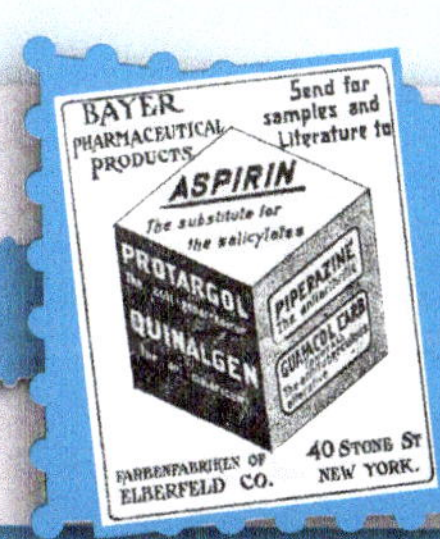

Glossary

chemical everything in the world is a chemical, or made up of chemicals

medicine a substance used to treat or prevent disease

scientists people who find out all they can about the world

Index